Do you know what opposites are?

How many questions can you answer?
It's fun to peek behind
the flap — to see if you
were right ...

PRICE/STERN/SLOAN
Publishers, Inc., Los Angeles

What is the opposite of
fast?

What is the opposite of cold?

What is the opposite of lost?

What is the opposite of
wet?

What is the opposite of
stop?

What is the opposite of big?

What is the opposite of in?

What is the opposite of fat?

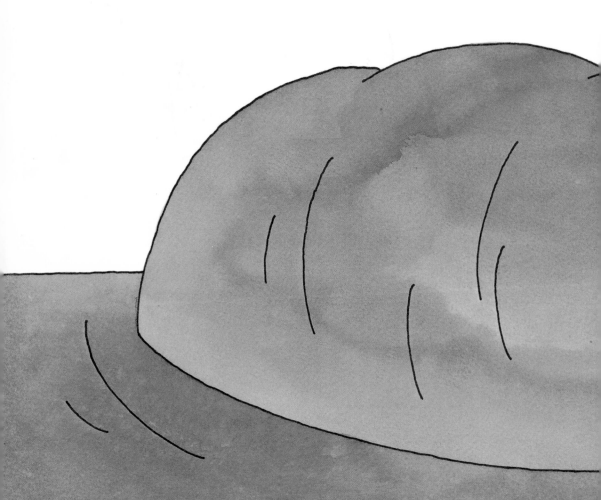

What is the opposite of
sad?

What is the opposite of
down?